THIS·BOOK·IS·A·GIFT
IN·MEMORY
·OF·

CYNTHIA·FALK·FINNEY

The Funny Little Woman

retold by Arlene Mosel
pictures by Blair Lent

PUFFIN BOOKS

The Funny Little Woman is based on a tale by Lafcadio Hearn.

Text copyright © 1972 by Arlene Mosel
Illustrations copyright © 1972 by Blair Lent

All rights reserved.

Unicorn is a registered trademark of Dutton Children's Books.

Library of Congress number 75-179046
ISBN 0-14-054753-3

Published in the United States by Dutton Children's Books,
a member of Penguin Putnam Inc.
375 Hudson Street, New York, New York 10014

Editor: Ann Durell
Manufactured in China
First Unicorn Edition 1986
37 38 39 40

Long ago, in Old Japan, there lived a funny little woman who liked to laugh, "Tee-he-he-he," and who liked to make dumplings out of rice.

One morning, as she was patting and shaping the rice flour, one of the dumplings started to roll. It rolled across the table; it rolled to the edge of the table, and then fell right to the earthen floor.

"Stop," cried the little woman. But the dumpling rolled and rolled until it rolled down a hole.

"Ungrateful dumpling," scolded the little woman, as she knelt and reached for it.

But just then the earth gave way, and head over heels she tumbled and tumbled

until she found herself on a most unusual road.
It was a hilly road lined with statues of the gods.

"My dumpling! My dumpling! Where is my
dumpling?" she shouted as she ran.

Soon she came to one of the statues.

"Jizo Sama, did you see my dumpling?"

"Yes, I saw your dumpling roll by three minutes ago, but you had better not follow it because the wicked *oni* live at the end of the road."

"Oh, tee-he-he-he," laughed the funny little woman. "I'm not afraid of the *oni*." And she kept running down the road crying, "My dumpling! My dumpling! Has anybody seen my dumpling?"

"I have," said a very stern Jizo. "It rolled by me just two minutes ago. But don't run after it, for you will surely meet a wicked *oni*."

"Oh, tee-he-he-he," laughed the little woman. "I'm not afraid of the wicked *oni*." And she ran even faster, shouting, "My dumpling! My dumpling! Has anybody seen my dumpling?"

Soon she came to another Jizo and asked: "Dear Jizo, have you seen my dumpling?"

"It rolled by just one minute ago, but hurry and hide behind me, for here comes a wicked *oni*!"

The wicked *oni* stopped and bowed to Jizo.

"Good day, Jizo Sama!"

And very politely, Jizo said, "Good day."

Sniff, sniff, sniff. "Jizo Sama," cried the wicked *oni*, "I smell the smell of humankind!"

"Oh," said Jizo, "you only smell the breeze off the river."

"No, no," said the wicked *oni*. "I smell the—"

"Tee-he-he-he." The little woman could not keep from laughing. "Tee-he-he-he."

Then the wicked *oni* put one large arm behind Jizo and pulled the little woman out!

"What are you going to do with the little woman?" asked Jizo. "You won't hurt her, will you?"

"Hurt her! I should say not," said the wicked *oni*. "I'm going to take her home and have her cook for all of us."

"Tee-he-he-he," laughed the little woman as the wicked *oni* took her down the road to a wide river. He put her into a boat and took her across the river to a strange house.

In the kitchen he gave her a large wooden paddle.

"Now this is how you must cook our rice," said the wicked *oni.* "First put one, just one grain of rice in this pot. Stir it with this magic paddle and you will soon have a potful."

"Tee-he-he-he," laughed the little woman. "That's easy."

And soon after the wicked *oni* left she tried it out. One grain of rice and then stir! And as she stirred the one grain became two, two became four, then eight, sixteen, thirty-two, sixty-four, one hundred and twenty-eight, two hundred and fifty-six — and the pot was full!

"Tee-he-he-he," she laughed. "What fun I shall have making rice dumplings."

The weeks and months passed as the little woman kept busy cooking rice for the wicked *oni*. (For *oni* eat more rice than most people!)

One afternoon she grew lonely for her little house and decided to return. First she tucked the magic paddle in her belt, then she went out the door. She looked to left and right — there were no *oni* to be seen.

She ran to the river, stopped, and looked behind—still there were no *oni*. Now, quietly she got into the boat; then away she went.

Since the river was wide, she had only reached the middle when the *oni* returned and found her missing.

Soon the *oni* were all on the bank watching her.

Now, because *oni* do not swim, they thought of a plan to stop her. All of them got on their knees and drank the water from the river!

When the little woman found the boat stuck in the mud, she was too frightened to laugh, so she jumped from the boat and began running. Her feet stuck in the mud, her hands stuck in the mud, and she fell in the mud!

"Tee-he-he-he, *tee-he-he-he, tee-he-he-he*," roared the *oni*. The little woman made a funny sight! Of course, when they laughed, all the water fell from their mouths back into the river, so the little woman jumped in the boat and away she went.

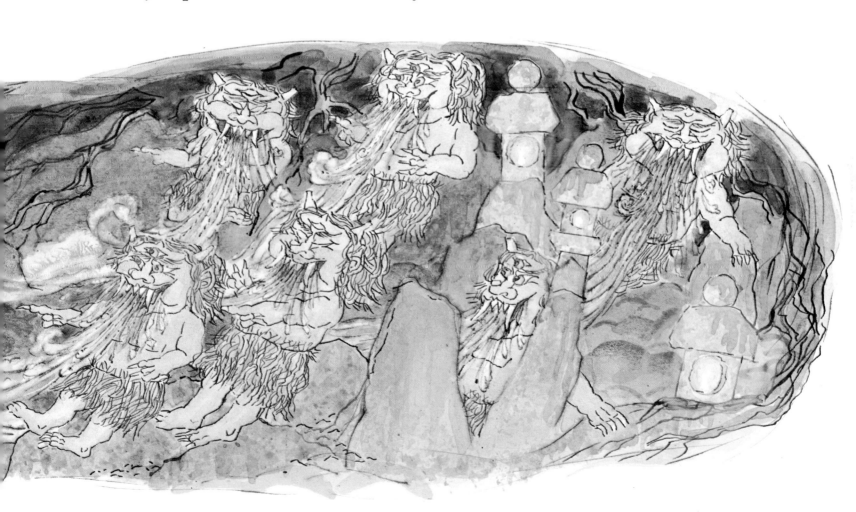

After that, the little woman was very happy, for, with her magic paddle, she could make more rice dumplings faster than ever. So she sold them and soon became the richest woman in all of Japan.

"Tee-he-he-he-he!"